Disney

THE
NUTCRACKER
AND THE
FOUR REALMS

To Beth, my prima ballerina forever
—C.G.

For my mom and dad, who supported my desire to make
art before I was any good at it. And for my wife,
who supports my desire to keep making art today.
—M.B.

Printed in the United States of America
First Hardcover Edition, September 2018

1 3 5 7 9 10 8 6 4 2
ISBN 978-1-368-02036-7
Library of Congress Control Number: 2018930676

FAC-034274-18215

Designed by Gegham Vardanyan

For more Disney Press fun, visit www.disneybooks.com

DISNEY
THE Nutcracker
AND THE
Four Realms

The Dance of the Realms

Foreword by MISTY COPELAND

Written by CALLIOPE GLASS • Illustrated by MARCO BUCCI

DISNEY PRESS

Los Angeles • New York

THE NUTCRACKER was the first ballet I ever performed with the San Pedro City Ballet. I was thirteen years old, living in San Pedro, California, and had been dancing for only eight months. I danced the coveted role of Clara and fell in love with performing, ballet, and *The Nutcracker*, all at once. The second production of *The Nutcracker* I performed in was Debbie Allen's *Hot Chocolate Nutcracker*. I was still a young dancer, only fourteen or fifteen years old, but sharing the stage with Debbie was yet another milestone in my early career. Each time I stepped on the stage to perform *The Nutcracker*, it solidified my love of this ballet. Just hearing the music makes you think of Christmas and wintertime.

Four years later, I performed *The Nutcracker* for the first time with my dream company, American Ballet Theatre in New York City. Throughout the course of my two-decade career, I've continued to perform this ballet, dancing just about every role, from Clara to a doll, a Spanish dancer to a marzipan shepherdess, and ultimately to the Sugar Plum Fairy. It never, ever gets old, largely because we dancers know that this ballet brings endless joy to those who come to see it.

For many people, *The Nutcracker* is a cornerstone of their ballet experience. I witness it every year when families fill the theaters and excitedly take their seats before the curtain goes up. The thrill of *The Nutcracker* can be found in many elements of the ballet. It's the breathtakingly dramatic music that pleasantly lingers in the ears, the flamboyant costumes and set designs that dazzle the eyes, and the memorable characters that make us laugh and cry. It is for these reasons and more that not only does this culturally iconic story bring generations of people together during the holidays, it holds an incredibly special place in my heart as the ballet that helped shape me as a ballerina and first sparked my love of the art.

When I first learned that Disney was working on a movie devoted to *The Nutcracker*, even if it didn't follow the story of the ballet to which I am accustomed, I was very interested. How could I not accept? To be a part of Disney's creation of *The Nutcracker and the Four Realms* is a dream. Lasse Hallström's vision is a beautiful marriage of two worlds: Disney and ballet.

I traveled to London immediately after completing a fall performance season with ABT to film the dance scene. The team of dancers and I worked with Liam Scarlett, an amazing choreographer who transformed the various Realms into wondrous, captivating lands filled with exquisite dancing characters. The first time I stepped on set, I felt as if I'd been transported to another time, another place. The space was so incredible and spectacular that it took a moment for it to sink in that this was the place where my portion of the story would be told.

Having the chance to tell a story through movement is one of my favorite things about dancing, as well as one of my favorite things about *The Nutcracker*. Dancing in this whimsical, yet dark, beautiful, and enchanting tale has given me the opportunity to bring people into this magical world on an even larger scale. Through my eyes, fingers, legs, and feet, I get to tell a story within a story in this spellbinding interpretation of *The Nutcracker*. So come along and join me on this fantastic adventure! Welcome to *The Nutcracker and the Four Realms*.

—Misty Copeland

T HE WORLD IS MADE
OF STORIES.

Some of them are happy, some
of them are sad, and all of them
beautiful in their own ways.

Watch and listen, dear ones,
and I'll tell you a story in
words and in dance.

Not so very long ago, in a land not terribly far from here . . .

A young girl named Clara received a gift. It was an intricate egg-shaped box, left for her by her mother, whom she missed terribly.

It was beautiful, but there was no key to open it.

Fortunately, that night was
Christmas Eve, a night that
opens many doors and reveals
many secrets. And Clara's
godfather, Drosselmeyer, was
having a splendid party, as he
did every year.

His sprawling home was
itself quite full of secrets and
doors—the kind of house
where lost keys might be
found. Clara asked her beloved
godfather where she might
look, and he showed her a path
to follow. All she had to do
was trust where her heart was
leading.

Clara's quest carried her
through a secret door and into
another world entirely—a
world of magic and surprise.

A world of Four Realms.

But when she entered this magical world, she found herself in a place that was battered, broken, and full of untold dangers. No sooner had Clara found her key than she'd lost it again— and nearly lost her life with it.

In the nick of time, Clara escaped and fled to a stunning palace with the help of a kind soldier. There, the beautiful Sugar Plum took Clara under her wing.

Clara considered herself an inventor, but she discovered something new about herself that day: she was also the princess of the Four Realms.

The folk of the Four Realms were so thrilled to meet Clara that they hosted a pageant in her honor.

"The pageant tells the story," Sugar Plum whispered, "of how your mother created our world."

And so Clara, breathless with the beauty of it, watched a story unfold in dance. A story she had never heard before.

A story about another inventor.

A *lonely* inventor.

This lonely inventor created
a grand Engine to bring into
being Realms of snowflakes,
flowers, sweets, and laughter.

And then, lacking companions, she took her beloved toys and tinkered with them until they came to life.

But one toy was very wicked: Mother Ginger. She wanted power over the Realms and would not live in peace with the others. Soon all the toys were at war!

A terrible battle raged—smoke and dust and fury—and all Four Realms were thrown into chaos.

As the battle unfolded onstage, Clara spotted one of Mother Ginger's villainous mice clutching a prop key. And it looked very familiar.

So that's where my key's gone! Clara thought. *Mother Ginger must have it.*

Beside her, Sugar Plum curled her dainty hand into a fist.

When the dust cleared at last, three Realms had triumphed over the terrible Mother Ginger. And yet . . . although the battle had been won, Mother Ginger still ruled the Fourth Realm.

The war was far from over.

"I hope you will be the one to finish it," Sugar Plum whispered, leaning close to Clara as the pageant ended. Her eyes were very bright.

Mother Ginger had Clara's key.
Mother Ginger was a threat
to the Four Realms. Clara
knew her duty as her mother's
daughter: Mother Ginger would
have to be defeated.

But Clara's battle with Mother Ginger did not unfold as prettily as the story in the pageant had. Something was strange; something was wrong; someone was lying. Clara felt it in her heart, and she was learning that her heart was not something she should ignore.

Clara got the key from Mother Ginger and made her way
back to the palace. She soon found herself in pitched battle
with none other than . . .

Sugar Plum!

And here is something to remember about stories, dear ones: they are all beautiful in their ways, but they are not always entirely *true*.

All along, the enemy of the Realms had been the beautiful and treacherous Sugar Plum.

The war had been her doing and hers alone—a selfish bid to rule the Realms.

A formidable villain indeed, the wicked Sugar Plum. But Clara—clever, brave, and stubborn—outdid her at the last. She used her mother's grand Engine and key to turn the evil fairy back into a doll.

Clara saved the Four Realms!

The Four Realms are made of stories, just like our world.

Watch and listen, dear ones: I have one more story to tell to you.

Some of it is happy, and some of it is sad—

And all of it is true.

Not so very long ago, in a land
not so terribly far from here . . .

A little girl who had lost her
mother found herself in a
magical realm.

And because she was clever,
and because she was kind, and
because she was brave . . .

Her story has a happy ending.